DESERT REPORT

DESERT REPORT

Book 3 in the Desert Series, proceeded by Desert Stones and Desert Trails

JUNE A. REYNOLDS
Illustrated By Clyde List

ReadersMagnet, LLC

Desert Report
Copyright © 2023 by June A. Reynolds

Published in the United States of America
ISBN   Paperback: 978-1-959761-84-6
ISBN   eBook: 978-1-959761-85-3

All rights reserved. No part of this publication may be reproduced, stored in a retrieval system or transmitted in any way by any means, electronic, mechanical, photocopy, recording or otherwise without the prior permission of the author except as provided by USA copyright law.

The opinions expressed by the author are not necessarily those of ReadersMagnet, LLC.

ReadersMagnet, LLC
10620 Treena Street, Suite 230 | San Diego, California, 92131 USA
1.619. 354. 2643 | www.readersmagnet.com

Book design copyright © 2023 by ReadersMagnet, LLC. All rights reserved.

Cover design by Kent Gabutin
Interior design by Dorothy Lee

TABLE OF CONTENTS

Preface 7
The Trail of Los Banos 10
God's Dogs 14
Juan Carlos Trail 17
Border Report from Lukeville 20
Dear Oregon, ... 22
Border Report from Sasabe 24
Cow-Killer Kirtchner 26
Wild West is Gone 30
Meanwhile, In the Movie Version. 31
Desert Saguaro 42
Murderous Visions 45
The Desert Full Moon 56
The Wall 57
The Unique Cactus Wren 64
Cactus Wren 66
Bird Count Report: Narrative 67
Crisis in Dog Patch 70
Concealed Carry 75
Smoke Signals 78
Desert Gems 90
The Solar Farm 91

PREFACE

It is hard for me to believe that we have been visiting Arizona for ten years now. The vast landscape swallows us up. The breeze moves us along pushing us this way and that, like the dust devil blowing up the dirt road.

And yet, here we are again after a long hiatus, at our base camp, still alive, having not gotten COVID yet, (knock on wood). Our strange journey began back on March 30, 2020 when we camped out past Darby Wells near Ajo, Arizona. We were in the desert and the only people that we saw from afar was the Border Patrol and the construction workers building a new mega-highway for roadrunners and trucks hauling steel plates out to the border wall. We were there a couple of days on Bates Well Road, minding our own business when we turned on the truck radio and heard that COVID-19 was in the state of Arizona.

DESERT REPORT

There was talk of closing the schools and shuttering all nonessential stores. Quarantine. We hung around the camp and for several days discovered Ajo lilies, birds, lizards, and jackrabbits. Finally, we left our desert camp and went back to civilization where all heck was breaking out about the pandemic on TV.

The situation did not get better and so we packed up the truck and left Tucson the day that Governor Doug Ducy officially closed the state of Arizona. All the hotels in the giant county of San Bernardino, California were closed, so we traveled far south to circumvent the whole county. There were many people marooned on the road—so many of them, that they were allowed to stay overnight in the rest stops. After four days we were back in Sherwood, Oregon where co-vidulty rates were a quarter of what they were in Arizona. As summer passed, we stayed hunkered in our home and 2021 came along with the promise of a vaccination in the spring. It was a long, trying winter. We got our COVID vaccine.

My daughter in Phoenix got married in April of 2021 so we carefully went back for a tentative trip. Everything was frozen in time. We experienced the ceremony and visited a few people with masks, outdoors. Then we traveled back to Oregon.

Now we are back in November 2021 through March 30 2022. COVID has faded and the delta variant has plateaued in Arizona. We got booster and flu shots. Now on the last days of November, the omicron virus is remotely threating our world.

So, this is my report on our Southwest experiences, both pre-COVID and in real-time. It is a collection of truth, facts, mythic tales, historic episodes, biographic sketches, and unadulterated poetry.

I know that our days are numbered and the dreams of the Wild West from Northwest through Southwest are being shattered and forgotten, so I'm here with my Desert Report.

THE TRAIL OF LOS BANOS

Normally we didn't hike with a guide, but in order to do this hike, we had to have one since it was very close to the Mexican border. The state park demanded it. At the trail head we parked our truck and got out our hiking gear. The trail guide was all over the parking lot, getting everyone ready to go. He was in a real rush and wanted us to hurry.

"We want to get going because of the angle of the sun," he shouted with a Spanish lilt to his voice. "We have good weather and want to get over the mountain at the right time. We will have to Go, Go, Go!"

I shook my head and said quietly, "What does the angle of the sun have to do with anything?" My husband just smiled and shrugged.

"We are hiking in the old Apache country of 1888. This also was the route of the Catholic Missionaries, such as Father Kino," the guide lectured. "Today, what he saw for the first time, uh, er. . ."

The hiking group was milling around and not really listening to him. They were taking selfies, packing their backpacks, modeling their new sun hats, and putting on sunscreen.

The guide coughed and finally got everyone's attention. "Does everyone have tinted lenses or sunglasses?" What followed was more scurrying around to get the right eye-ware. Finally, the line formed and people were ready to hike.

Up the trail about ten steps there was a sign that proclaimed "The Trail of Los Banos." The guide ignored the sign by passing it by and lead the group up the first switchbacks up the first hill. Later on, I approached the guide and asked him what "Los Banos" meant, but he suddenly could not understand English and he told me mostly in sign language to just get off the trail and go behind a bush.

The trail rose up the mountain in a series of switchbacks and stairways. We saw some beautiful cardinals and their multicolored cousins, the pyrrhuloxia, leaping and flying from tree to tree above our heads. They were actually following us up the trail until we reached a pool of water called Smith Tank. There was a small herd of range cows on the other side of the pool, sucking up the water. We had a quick lunch and were soon back on the trail again. We wound our way around about twenty protruding rocks of granite and then started up a large fold in the earth. The trail once again had six switchbacks to the top and finally we were on top of the ridge, looking to the southwest, right into the sun. In no time at all, we descended to the desert floor and our trail was now a distinct two-track road. The traces of road unfolded like an unspooled ribbon. But soon it straightened out. The heat waves were sweltering like unfolding waves. The guide shouted, "There it is: Los Banos!"

In front of us on the two-track was a pool of water, deeply beckoning us. It was shimmering and shiny in the afternoon sun.

"Water!" shouted one of the mouthy kids.

"An optical illusion." Said the other outfitted guy.

"A mirage," said his wife.

"Si, Si," said our guide. "You get it. You are very smart! When the Catholic Priest, Father Kino, came over this ridge in the 1600s, he and his men had never seen this sight. The desert was very sandy and barren and the mirage looked like a large water body. They had been traveling for many days. They were hot and tired and raced to the Los Banos to drink and bathe. The closer they came, the farther the pools were ahead of them. They exhausted themselves."

Sure enough, as we hiked another mile, the illusion would travel ahead of us. We were becoming bedraggled ourselves. The sun was beating on our heads. All of our water was gone.

The guide stopped. "See that bush in the distance? That is the end of the trail."

"Yay!" said one of the mouthy kids. "I can't wait to jump in!" He already had his shirt off and started looking a little pink.

Our pace picked up for a while and the mirage came and went. The little boy would run ahead, then see there was more trail to go, and he would get bedraggled. I thought of those Spanish priests and conquistadores who came through this country. *What a harsh life!*

When we approached the bush, I discovered it was a huge tree, growing in the bottom of a twenty-foot-wide wash. *The tree of life!*

"Where is this wash you promised we could swim in?" demanded the young boy.

"This is it," laughed the leader. "But it is only full during the monsoons."

We rested for a while, then we climbed aboard a van to go back to the trail head and our cars. The hike on the Los Banos trail was six miles long one way.

GOD'S DOGS

I wanted to tell you about God's dogs. Humans call them coyotes. The creator, I'itoi, says they are his dogs. After all "Dog" is "God" spelled backwards. They are wildly free-run canines who really don't have a fancy-free life, out there in the desert. They stick to business most of the time, they cover a lot of ground in a day and night. But once in a while, they are curious. If there is anything out of place, they will examine it. They will crawl under a car that is randomly parked. They will test out a new mailbox. One day, there was a new dog in the neighborhood. The coyote watched it dancing around and loudly barking. He then started doing the same movement and they pranced around like that for over an hour with a fence between them. The domesticated and the wild: mirror images of each other!

Coyotes do not follow a human's trail. They will cross the trail and go their own way, snaking this way and that. They will follow the same pattern day in and day out, to not get lost. They walk a parallel path to a fence or road. The only time they ever travel straight ahead is when buckshot it being pumped into their backside! I know because I was driving along one day on a dirt road, and out shot a coyote from the ditch in front of the car. He rocketed in a straight line galloping along. He had a ruffle of thick, winter fur on his back which was flapping in the movement. I almost ran over that coyote, but providence guided him, with a leap clear across the street and into the ditch.

Beauty is not lost on the coyote. He poops on the prettiest rock on the trail. He has been known to leave his calling card on a beautiful flowering rattlesnake cactus. The rest of the time, he hides his poop by scratching sand

and rock over it, neatly. Because of his strange habits, he is known widely as a trickster with a sense of humor. I think we are largely projecting this on the animal, but it makes the story so much more interesting. Like all of God's animals, the coyote gets thirsty. They have a keen nose for water. Don't yell at them too hard when they bite into your water system. Don't chase them too hard when they dig in the clay in your driveway. This is all part of nature. We need to get along better with nature.

As a Tohono O'Odham native, I have decided to let my dogs run free on the streets in the town with the coyotes. The smart dogs are learning coyote ways. My dogs are sort of indigenous dogs with a lively sense of being, who can come home any time to a bowl of dry dog food and water, that is, if a javelina has not gotten to it already.

JUAN CARLOS TRAIL

Juan Carlos lived near Valenzuela Road.
It was an old wagon road used by the U.S. Calvary forty to fifty years before Juan Carlos came to this area. He reckons he came to this place in around 1920. His hacienda and corrals were on the high part of his land, close to the wagon trail. There was a well out back where there was an artesian slip in the rock. From there, the land slanted downhill and beyond that was a strange bowl of earth which was in grassland. No water-sucking buffel grass, like we have today, but a very fine sort of grass.

While the rest of the ranchers bought bricks of hay from California, Juan Carlos harvested hay from his desert grassland. He hand-dug the weeds out of the rocky soil and tried to divert water into the bowl without flooding it. He harvested hanks of hay and tied them with bits of rope, twisted brush, yarn, or even hay, itself. He would bring his donkey back to the paddock, all bristly with the hanks of hay tied with brilliant colors. The trail goes to the field, but goes no farther. The field is still there, along with the old adobe house and the paddocks built with old mesquite wood and live, bristly ocotillo stalks.

Oh, for the good old days before COVID! Then-President Donald Trump declared a national emergency as "hordes" of people from the south were going to breach the border. In the early days, things were so simple.

BORDER REPORT FROM LUKEVILLE

Northbound from Mexico to the United States, February 15, 2019, Day one of the National Emergency:
6:00 a.m. Marcella Sisters are first in line to go over the border. They have one hour to drive forty miles to Ajo. They must go through another checkpoint, to get to their café.
6:30 a.m. Two RVs of Americans. Raining in Rocky Point.
6:35 a.m. A van load of Mexican ladies going to La Siesta to do their maid duties.
8:00 a.m. A truck load of cheaply made culverts going to the Organ Pipe National Monument.
Southbound from the United States to Mexico
9:35 a.m. Vanload of students from University of Arizona with their professor to study volcanic shields.
11:45 a.m. Three RVs going to Rocky Point.
12:30 p.m. Vanload of Government workers going to the Lukeville Café.
1:50 p.m. Tohono O'odham family going to a relative's funeral.

Northbound from Mexico to the United States
2:00 p.m. Truck and Trailer full of horses going to the Tucson Rodeo.
2:15 p.m. Government workers back from Lukeville Café.
Southbound from the United States to Mexico
4:00 p.m. Mexican maids coming back from work.
4:15 p.m. Mexican lettuce pickers from Yuma going home for the weekend.
5:00 p.m. Old, beat-up camper going to Rocky Point.
5:25 p.m. Marcella Sisters going home after their shift.
Gates closed at 6:00 p.m.
November 27, 2019

October 17, 2019

DEAR OREGON,

Greetings from Dog Patch, Arizona! Thank you for your last rainstorm. We got it via air mail and it has made our state very gray for three whole days in a row. Of course, by the time we got it, there was not much water to wring out of the towel. The gray cotton balls of clouds just skidded over each other through the sky, making cloud watching fun but rain watching rather frustrating since it rained only at night. I must say the thunder and ball lightening was spectacular and got our attention.

On the other hand, the bursage bushes are turning from crackling-dry to short green ends for the bunnies to nibble. There is hope for perennials to start sprouting and flowering in the spring, and the saguaros—well they will take anything: water drops, deluge, mist, fog, or sweat.

We have not been without our casualties, though. A roadrunner got hit in the head by the first rain drop. He looked up with his beak open and started to drown as two more drops went into his mouth. But not to worry! I ran right out and did roadrunner CPR and he is back to full breathing.

And speaking of migration, later on that day, there was a mild drum beat of tiny hooves, vibrating the desert. A thousand javelinas came marching in a long line parade down from Cat Mountain and Golden Gate to play in our ever-widening clay lined puddles in our dirt road.

All in all, this has been a great weather event. It is predicted that we will have two more days of your Oregon weather, filling up the puddles and freshening the air and desert plants. However, please don't send your next storm, thank you—we are not ready for the snow!

Sincerely, Arizona Annie

BORDER REPORT FROM SASABE

Day 7 of the National Emergency at the border. Thursday, February 21, 2019. Sasabe is eighty miles southeast from Lukeville on the East Side of the Tohono O'odham Native Lands, were the Babaquivari Mountains swing down to the border.

Southbound from the United States

6:00 a.m. Thirty-three degrees and very windy. Aravaca woman waiting at the border. She is going to the dentist.

6:30 a.m. Truck-load of goats, being sold to a Mexican rancher near El Sasabe. Permits and papers up-to-date.

7:00 a.m. Two vanloads and a jeep. A quail hunting party with hunting permits for the Sonoran region.

Northbound from Mexico

8:30 a.m. Truck load of avocados. Papers in order.

1:30 p.m. Empty truck which hauled the goats.

2:35 p.m. Roadrunner and his mate make a rush at the twenty-foot fence. Two attempts to fly over are made by the male. He succeeds. As we watch and laugh, the female skitters by us, right at our feet.

3:00 p.m. Aravaca woman coming home from the dentist.

5:35 p.m. Quail hunting party returns. They did not get their limit. Comments are made that Mexico needs more coyotes to keep down the hordes of jackrabbits in the desert.

6:00 p.m. Port of entry closed.

Feburary 22, 2019
5:30 a.m. Open Gates
Northbound from Mexico

7:20 a.m. Snake catcher coming home to the United States after a night of catching rattlers in the south side of the Babaquivari foothills. Frightening inspection.

6:00 p.m. No other north- or southbound entries. Port of entry closed.

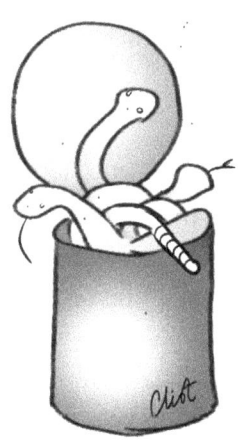

COW-KILLER KIRTCHNER

Near Hidden Valley Ranch, AZ, 1956

The air was clear and cold as the sun glowed over the Rincon Mountains that morning. The men and boys each with a bird gun were lined up and were going to fan out together in a southeast direction. Everyone moved off together, looking for the quail. The fan soon disappeared as the men were walking faster than the boys. The boys were paired up but were scattered all over the desert. We wound off and on the main trail, then we totally left the trail and the direction of the hunt.

So here was me and Charlie—out in the desert. Yep. Two Tucson boys out in the wilds with a wide, up-close view of the lofty Catalina Mountains. This was to be our manly rite of passage out on a quail hunt with the Tucson Rod and Gun Club. We were lounging on some boulders in a wash, having a smoke break.

I took a long drag and then exhaled. Pot shots could be heard in the distance. "You know, Charlie, I don't think I've seen a living thing out here."

Charlie winked at me and said, "I think they have killed them all." He started to walk down the wash, looking around to see if he could flush out any quail. I followed him and used the butt of my gun as a walking stick. Charlie stopped and turned to me. "You know, Carl, if Crayola wanted a new color, they should make 'Sandy.' The desert kids would use lots of sticks of that crayon."

I shook my head. "I wouldn't know. I'm colorblind." My coke bottle lenses flashed light all around the wash.

Charlie and I were seniors at Amphi High School which was a very modern, progressive school in those times. Everything was planned and categorized. The school was even partners with the Rod and Gun Club for this event and we were members of this group as we were fatherless teens to be lifted up by the bootstraps by these prosperous businessmen, whoever they were. The school even had us categorized; Charlie was on a workingman's track and I was on the college track.

Suddenly, on the bank of the wash above us, there was a lot of bird cheeping and fluttering of wings. We rushed up the side of the wash, not worried in the least that we were eroding the soil on the bank. By the time we got up out of the wash, there were birds fluttering this way and that. We sprayed the ground, machine-gun style, but I didn't think we hit a single bird. We reloaded and shot some more.

DESERT REPORT

Then we heard a grunt and a thud. Something large had hit the ground! We waded this way and that through the cactus and brush and there, under a Palo Verde was a huge milk cow! She was grunting and moaning and then she was silent. Her milk bag was shot a million times over. The milk and blood were a gruesome sight. We grabbed some Palo Verde limbs and laid them over the cow then innocently walked back out to where the quail were fluttering. We sprayed the desert with birdshot. This time around, we found a few dead birds and clipped them on our catch line. Then we found the main trail with our party coming back to regroup. It was hot out and the party decided to call it a day.

"We call this meeting of the Tucson Rod and Gun Club to order," announced Kerry Concannon.

I was summoned to this meeting on the phone by the president, himself. I looked around for Charlie, but there was not hide nor hair of him anywhere. *Oh man, I bet the rancher found that milk cow and by now she is probably dead. I am going to be in hot water.*

"Let's have a moment of mourning for the Birdy family." Said Kerry. We all bowed our heads and I tried to shift a few seats over to the aisle for a quick get-away.

"Amen," said Kerry. We all sat down. "We had an unfortunate accident at the ranch last week," continued Kerry. "Although the quail kill was successful, there was an incident in which someone blew the milk bag right off of a milk cow! Mr. Birdy found the cow on Thursday and she was dead. We, of course, are reimbursing Mr. Birdy for the cow. After some investigation, we found out that it was Charlie Kirtchner who did it. I move that we blackball that S.O.B. It's up to you, fellers." He held the glass fishbowl in one hand and passed it over to the next man. With his other hand, he grabbed out a black marble from a plastic container, and put it in the fishbowl. It clanked loudly.

When the bowl got to me, I pretended to do something with it. Luckily, by then no one was paying attention to what was going on. By the end, there were three marbles still in the plastic container.

"That does it," said Kerry Concannon. "Charlie Kirtchner is blackballed out of the Tucson Rod and Gun Club. May we always remember 'Cow Killer Kirtchner' and observe more gun safety when hunting on the range."

I stood up and walked swiftly out of the lodge. I never went back to those meetings again and in fact, I never saw Cow Killer Kirtchner ever again.

DESERT REPORT

Wild West is Gone

Wide open spaces and fencing replaces
The places we used to gallop and run.
Wild actions restrain and the rules are so plain.
There's no striking out, to gambol about
To have an adventure by horse or by foot.
The days of the Wild West are over and gone.
The glory days have seen their last dawn.
So, let's lift a pint at this pitiful sight.
Of the nights and the days so long.
Home on the Range is over and gone.
The rolling valley looks all the same.
The land is a'groom, no more animal room.
There's too many houses all crowded like louses
And the streets all have Wild West names.

MEANWHILE, IN THE MOVIE VERSION...

Jerry Jeff Burdge was a cowboy hero. He worked the ranches in West Texas and always got his stock to market on time. One fateful day, outside of Tucson, Arizona, there was a storm a'brew'en up on the mountain pass. He watched those clouds a'boil'en up there. He moved his herd up into the foothills then went down to an elbow in the dry river bed where a tribe of Indians were camped. He had to warn them. From below, they could not see the black billowing clouds as he saw them on the flat desert or through the pass. They had no perspective from their position. He told those natives to move up and out of the curved floodplain. They moved their kids, and horses, stock, and some of their tents, but before long, a huge swath of water was thundering down the canyon. Jerry Jeff and many of the Native men were swept away down the wash.

Meanwhile, In the Movie Version...

Photo by Ed Davenport

John Wayne hopped off the private plane at the Tucson airport and turned to his assistant. "Where are my bags? The assistant ran to the baggage hatch to look for the bags. Five minutes later, he came back. He was sweating in the relentless dry heat.

"Uh, sir, I cannot find them."

John Wayne was furious. "Well, if that don't beat all—You are fired!"

Jerry Jeff was in a hospital bed. A doctor looked at the chart. "Nurse what happened to this man?"

The nurse said, "He was swept down a river in a flood. His lungs are full of water. Boulders rolled over him and under him, so he has multiple bruises and factures in his limbs and ribs. He crawled out of the wash with a couple of other Indians and they sat in the desert for a day, before the rest of the Indians found them, so he also has heat exhaustion."

Meanwhile, In the Movie Version. . .

John Wayne was being fitted in his costume in his little rock house off of Aklam Road. He was sweating and had a dry mouth. John looked at the costumer. "The shirt fits, but not this vest," he said as he popped the button. He laid the vest on a chair and walked to the bright sunny open door.

Photo by Ed Davenport
"Wait!" called the costumer. "I need that shirt."

"Too bad," said John Wayne, without looking back. "I don't have any clean clothes."

Jerry Jeff Burge slowly lifted his head off the pillow and painstakingly sat up. He was in a hospital gown. His ribs felt bruised and his chest ached. He wondered if he had been in a stampede. By the light of a streetlight outside, he found his pants but no shirt. Then he laid down to rest.

Meanwhile, In the Movie Version. . .

John Wayne strode across the little compound and went to the corral. "Which horse is mine?" he asked the stable boy.

The boy grinned. "That white one over there."

"Too old," said John Wayne. His eyes went over the herd. "I want that chestnut one over there with some spunk."

"But, uh. . ." hesitated the boy.

"No buts about it," he said as he marched over to look at the cattle coral.

The nurse came in to give Mr. Burge his pain pill. "Holy Moses!" she exclaimed as she pulled the blanket off of two pillows. Jerry Jeff was gone.

Meanwhile, In the Movie Version...

John Wayne looked at the herd in the corral. They looked more like milk cows rather than range cows. "How the Holy Heck are these cows going to turn into stampedin' devils?" he groused out loud to no one.

The script girl came over to him. "Haven't you heard? These are just background cows. The script has changed too. Now you are going to save an Indian camp from a wash-out during a monsoon storm."

"But I don't know how to swim!" he wailed.

Jerry Jeff hobbled down the street, dressed in his torn pants and hospital gown. It was dark, but the moon was rising. He saw a late bus and waved to the driver as he limped across the street.

"Where ya'all go'en?" said the driver, as he watched the hospital gown blowing in the breeze.

"As far to the edge of town as this change will take me," said Jerry Jeff as he emptied his pockets.

The driver gave him a twenty-four-hour pass. Jerry Jeff nodded. He sat down in the bus seat in anguish.

Meanwhile, In the Movie Version...

Sloshing around in a wash filled by two tanker trucks and a garden hose, John Wayne was pretending to be carried downstream with a rock rolling in back of him and an Indian floating beside him. He grabbed the Indian and yelled, "I'll save you!"

Jerry Jeff finally got back to the ranch. One of the younger cowboys welcomed Jerry at the gate. He brought his horse, but he was in no shape to ride it yet. So, they slowly walked the two-track with their horses. After a few weeks of sitting around the bunkhouse, he was able to saddle up again in time for the cattle drive into town.

Meanwhile, In the Movie Version...

John Wayne sat stoically on his horse with Golden Gate Mountain in the background.

"Cut!" said the director.

"By the way," said John Wayne. "I've got a car pick'en me up here and driving me to Ghost Ranch in town."

"But you're paid up at Loma Linda for three months!" said the director.

"Can't stay there." said John. "There's a rattler under the back porch and I need a gin and tonic."

Photo by Ed Davenport

Meanwhile, the ranch hands had been gathering up the cattle from different ranges and had them all milling around in the corral. Jerry Jeff was pretty worried about his horse. She was getting older and this would probably be her last round-up. On the last day, they headed high up into the Catalinas to drive the last herd down to the ranch. By afternoon, they were at the base of Flat Iron, flushing the yearlings out like quail around the rocks.

Jerry Jeff rode his horse above the base of the rocks to make sure all the cattle were gathered up. Sure enough, there were six cows hovering in a ravine. "They are to the left of that ironwood," he yelled down to the cowboys. The men below whistled and bounded around the rocks to the ravine.

Jerry's horse gave out a surprised whinny. Jerry looked up, and there was a puma! Fat rounded face, furry paws, round, long tail, green eyes . . . ready to spring! The horse bolted upward and Jerry reigned it around, but when the horse came down, the rocky trail crumbled under her hooves! Jerry Jeff had farmed with a wagon and tractor long enough to know it was time to jump off to the wall of the cliff. He could hear the horse screaming as it flew off the other side. Jerry Jeff fell like a limp doll and laid there, blacked out.

The puma looked at the fallen horse and leapt down the bank to the trail. He passed Jerry's body and rapidly made his way down the ravine.

Next thing Jerry knew, he was looking into the eyes of his boss. "Whoa there, Jerry, don't get up just yet. Easy does it. I knew you were still up here when I saw your horse go'a fly'en off the cliff." He hoisted Jerry onto the horse, draping him on his belly over his horse. They rode slowly down the trail to his horse, below.

Meanwhile In the Movie Version...

"Well. Hi there, cowboy," purred Marilyn Monroe.

They were in the Ghost Ranch bar with other luminaries from the 1950s.

"Well, hi there, pretty lady," drawled John Wayne. His slurped the rest of his gin and tonic and raised his glass to the bartender for another.

Marilyn pressed on. "Aren't you going to buy me a drink?"

"Ah, sure, what are you drinking?" He reached for her empty glass and held it up for the bartender.

"Martini," she whispered. "What are you thinking?"

"I'm thinking about the shootout at the OK Corral that I have to do tomorrow..."

The rancher slowly slid Jerry off of his horse. "Do you think you've got any broken bones?" he said as he looked Jerry over top to bottom.

"No, I feel banged up and my old broken bones are hollering a bit, but I've got to get over to my horse. I can hear her." Sure enough, the horse was barely alive, with broken bones splintering off in odd, sickening ways. The horse raised up her head, with her wild eyes showing much white. She was making death toll whinnying sounds.

Jerry slumped down beside his dying horse. "We have to put her out of her misery, but my rifle is under her." Without thinking, the rancher handed him his pistol.

"No no, that won't do. I need a bigger gun. A rifle," said Jerry with tears in his eyes.

Another person came up to his side. It was the Rancher's daughter with her rifle. Her soft brown caring eyes looked at him steady as she held out the gun. It was done in two shots. All was quiet.

Meanwhile In the Movie Version. . .

John Wayne was striding down the dusty street of Tombstone. His costume was a perfect fit and the Marshall badge was all shiny and bright in the relentless sun. The armorer for the movie was buffing up a black gun. "Here sir," he said to John as he carefully handed it over.

This is just a little bitty old gun," grumbled John. "I need a big gun—a rifle in fact, so it will show up on screen."

"But this is the authentic, historically right gun that the Marshall used. . ."

"Well, get me the biggest historical right rifle you can find!" John snapped.

Jerry Jeff was finally healed and got his kit ready for the long drive to the stockyard in town where they would be loading up the cows in the cattle cars. Sophia, the rancher's daughter, loaned him her horse. She was already training another two year old for the cattle drives next year.

Jerry led the drive this year as they moved the massive swarm of cows over the desert. Monsoon season was over so they crossed the dry washes and finally the river which was empty, except for a rivulet which refreshed the cows for only a moment.

The gathering of cows swarmed back up onto the desert. Soon they were following the railroad tracks right into the livestock pens. The fattening, gathering, and driving was over for this year. The cowboys would have a night on the town at the saloon and then tomorrow, a long trek back to the ranch.

Meanwhile in the Movie Version. . .

"This screening looks like a cattle call," groused John Wayne. He was back in downtown Tucson at a very large movie theater. The ticket holders for the event snaked all the way around the block. John was quickly slipped around to a backstage door. They went through the blackened theater and sat down for some makeup and costume changes. Soon John was standing in the wings near the stage manager. John recognized the man who used to be one of the movie grips. "Why are you not on location anymore?" asked John.

"Oh, I've got five kids and I can't be out on set anymore."

"Hmmm, that figures," said John.

The announcer appeared on stage. There was polite applause. "Welcome to our first screening of 'The Pride of Western Man.' Without further ado, presenting the star of the show: John Wayne!"

The crowd went wild as John sauntered proudly to center stage. He took the mic from the announcer. "Waall," he drawled "I'm glad you came to the show and heck, let 'er roll!" He strolled back to the wings, took off his black hat and placed it on the stage manager's head. The theater owner whisked him away to a private viewing booth.

At the Airport:

On the tarmac, John Wayne was mobbed by fans and reporters. Flashbulbs exploded. John tried to get one last look at Golden Gate Mountain looming in the haze. There it was, purple on the horizon. He would remember it always.

Someone was shouting in his left ear: "So just *who* is the 'Pride of the West' in your new movie? Is it you, John Wayne?"

John Wayne shook his head. "No, you got it all wrong, Son. It is not about me. I'm just a caricature, you know, a cartoon."

"So who is the hero of the west or is it a spirit we cannot see because. . ."

"The pride of the west are the people that live here," snapped John. He just wanted to fly home to California and sit by his swimming pool, alone.

A movie critic pushed in to John's right. "But who do you think the screenwriter based his character on?"

John thought, "*Why don't these eggheads do some real research?*"

Then John Wayne beamed and blurted out: "Jerry Jeff Burdge."

And, fade to black, roll credits.

DESERT SAGUARO

March 25, 2022

I really don't want to boast, but for eight years, I've been a ghost.

Clicking and clacking 'a rattle-tat-tacking in wild windy lands, brittle as toast.

With pride I bust, I'm from the upper crust.
Kings and Queens of desert, from ground colored rust.
Before I was stanch in a forest reliant,
Green giants sticking up so proud and defiant.

Head of white crowns, each spring, fruits I wore,
'Till the fruits turned red in the sunset gore.

Then, of course, I was a silver screen star.
In a blockbuster western in desert so far.
John Wayne dashed through on a wild golden horse,
I had a cameo in the credits, of course.

At seventy-five years, I grew arms from my chest.
And a mother owl feathered her nest.

DESERT REPORT

The winters got cold, my arms swayed down toward
the ground,
We all did sway in a dance with no sound.
We were frozen in our dance for several years,
Until it got too dry, much to our fears.
We all became ghosts, one by one, in sun.
Our lives were happy—we had decades of fun.

MURDEROUS VISIONS

Yin and Yang

Thump thump swish. . . . they dragged her down the hallway kicking and screaming. Our cat-naps were rudely interrupted.

"Winnie, you really didn't have to throw your food tray at the wall," said the orderly in the hall. Keys clanked in the door and rattled open a few inches.

"Gol, darn it!" snarled Winnie. "You sar' him. That man is a beast!"

Three humans burst through the door. Two orderlies and Winnie all wrapped in white. The second orderly had a tight grip on Winnie's kicking legs and he gently laid her on the ground. The first orderly said, "There now, I want you to calm down and think about what you have done. If we see that you are still, we will come in and take the straitjacket off. I will try and get you some dinner, but I'm not promising anything."

"You saw him. It is his fault not mine," protested Winnie, weakly.

"I didn't see anyone, Winnie. Did you think you saw someone at the wall?" asked the second orderly.

In a low voice, the first orderly whispered, "Don't put ideas in her head now. . ."

Winnie laid there as the orderlies left and locked the door. As soon as the door clicked, our mistress made awful noises and spun around on the floor like a dying horse. It went on for so long it was scary and we hid in dark places. Her energy waned and she went to sleep. My brother Yang padded near her and smelled her head. I approached after a few moments and could tell she was still breathing. By nightfall, the first orderly came into the apartment and took her out of the white thing called a straightjacket. He got her up off the floor and onto the couch and gently said, "No more throwing your food tray at the wall, Winnie. You upset everyone so much that now you cannot go back to the cafeteria. That is not right, Winnie."

Winnie's voice crackled, "Uh huh. Anything you say sir."

We looked expectantly at the orderly with our pale blue eyes. He noticed us and went over to the table and poured some dry cat food in our bowl and then left.

Winnie

When I woke up again, I slowly sat up and looked around the room. The slot windows near the ceiling were showing the sun to be around noon. You notice these things much more when you live alone. My Siamese cats approached me with an aloof air and purred. They were nonjudgmental and kind. I loved them for that. I scratched them behind the ears and smoothed their fur.

"I am so hungry." I said out loud. Then I looked at my cats. "Oh! I bet you are too!" I jumped up, then sat back down. Then I got up again and limped over to the cat's bowl and poured in the food. Time went on but no one came to open the door and let me go to the cafeteria. Finally, we heard footsteps and someone slid the tray in the slot under the door. We watched the sun move through the three high windows and soon it got dark. I could have turned on the light, but I did not.

When I was young, I thought everyone was the same: religious, good, honest, and smart. My father was a minister and everyone we knew were just good people. Then I met a man who was also rich. He was a doctor and he would take me to the opera in fancy clothes and a fancy car. We went to parties at mansions. It seemed like a perfect life. After we married and moved away from my parents, I found out really fast that there were also many, many bad people: people who do bad things to people, and cheat, lie, and steal. They would call you names, be unkind, or rob you. People were so miserable that they would drink and take drugs, even in the Depression. My husband became an addict to cocaine and I came down with tuberculous, maybe because I was always bumming cigarettes from everyone. My husband became a shell of a man and I moved to Arizona to clear my lungs. The people I was around at home and at work were all interested in having a fun time, playing cards, drinking, smoking, and entertaining men. What has happened to me all these years?

Suddenly, on the wall, just a little bit under the ornate picture of my mother and father, there was Sammy, my closest girlfriend, just a few years younger than me. She was just staring at me. I took a deep breath, and said, "Hi Sammy! How are you doing?"

She frowned at me and kept staring.

I wanted to reach out to her. "I have missed you so much. Remember when we went to Mexico? Just the two of us?"

She put her hands on her hips and just kept staring.

I got up to turn on a light. But before I could, she screamed, "You killed me! You chopped me up and stuffed me in a trunk!"

"It was not my fault!" I yelled as I threw my half-eaten food tray at her face. She disappeared and potatoes and gravy slid down the wall.

I cried myself to sleep on the sofa.

Yin and Yang

After a few days of trays being thrown at the wall and Winnie yelling at people that were not there, a large food mural was splattered all over the wall. Us cats were in seventh heaven. Winnie took all the portraits of the family off the wall and the green trays were scattered this way and that on the floor. The chicken gravy and corn were better than the dry old cat food and we always approved of the fish. Yang, my brother even ate the carrots.

One day, the lazy the housekeeper who had skipped a few days came in and gasped in horror at the tasteful display. More humans in white coats came to talk at Winnie Ruth. They talked and she shouted.

Winnie

Winter was upon us and afternoons and evenings were very dark. I kept the lights on, just to keep the visions of people appearing on the wall. I was trying to keep my mind off the past, and was doing pretty well, when the howling wind knocked off the power. The cats came close to me in the darkness. A tray slid under the door. I knocked around in the dark and found the tray. I was very hungry. I ate the potatoes and gravy. Suddenly, there was Happy Jack Halloran smiling at me. His eyes were shining, despite the dark.

"Hi Honey!" he said in a most insincere way. "I'm home!"

"Don't you 'honey' me!" I said. "You were hanging off Sammy and oogling Agnes at the same time last night."

"Oh Winnie, don't be mad at me," he drawled at me like a Texan. "You are my first choice."

I saw this as a golden opportunity. "Then let's get married. Leave your wife and move in with me.

"Now you know I can't do that, Winnie, my money is all tied up with my wife," he said smoothly.

"Leave your wife and start over," I demanded.

"I put you up in your own house, darlin,'" he smoozed.

I cleared my throat. "With a leaky sink and a broken refrigerator. In the meantime, you buy your wife a racehorse!"

He put on his Cheshire Cat grin. "Well we must all keep up with appearances," he said with his gold teeth gleaming, despite the darkness.

My anger flooded the room, once again like it did on that fateful day. I flung my food tray at him as he danced across the wall and into the arms of Sammy.

"He loves me now," declared Sammy.

"No, he loves me!" screeched Agnes who jumped down from one of the slot windows. I grabbed the lamp, yanking it out of the socket and flung it at the wall at all three of them.

"I shot you gals in self-defense!" I shouted "You were attacking me and we were fighting. I am going to be hanged for something Jack is responsible for. He removed the evidence. The trunks were his plan." I felt dizzy as I fell back on the couch.

Suddenly, the lights came on. The murderous visions vanished and I was in a quiet room with my cats. I looked at my cats who stared back at me expectantly. "Okay, I was Happy Jack's second choice. Those girls were just his third and fourth choice."

Yin and Yang

The cute little apartment was in shambles during the light of day. Winnie sat on the couch with us purring in her lap. The humans came in again and talked about punishing Winnie. They said that if this happened again, they would take her cats away. The humans marched out to look for the housekeeper.

She petted us and cooed, "Don't worry, my dears, they will never, ever take you away from me. I will protect you."

But she didn't.

Philip (and Anthony)

I don't know how it happened, but when I was about eight or nine, we somehow came to be in custody of two Siamese cats. My Dad brought them home from work in a gunny sack slung low over his back. He brought them right into the living room and laid the sack on the floor with the top of the sack opened. Slowly the cats crept out of the sack. One was big and the other was thin and small.

"I get the big one!" shouted Anthony. He grabbed at the cat, but the cat dashed away to hide behind the curtains.

"Go slow, there Buckaroos," Dad warned. "These cats have been through a lot of crazy and we will have to train them. They were Winnie Ruth Judd's cats from the looney bin downtown."

I could not believe my ears. "You mean the Trunk Murderer?"

"Really?" exclaimed my Mom. "Siamese cats are all the rage right now. They come from Siam, boys, clear across the Pacific Ocean and these are celebrity cats too."

I slowly wormed my way on my belly across the rug towards the little cat. She had one blue eye and one green eye. I looked her straight in the face and she looked back. I could tell she was an older cat, but she seemed very friendly in a scaredy-cat way.

Anthony had his cat cornered by the door and he grabbed him. He got really stiff as Anthony picked him up and the cat started hissing and spitting.

Mom and Dad directed us boys to bring our cats into the kitchen. Dad got a bag of dry cat food and Mom got some old cracked bowls. As soon as the cats saw the food, they calmed down and started eating. I petted mine on the back as she gulped down her food.

Winnie

For three days, I sat there. My cats were gone, but the visions I saw were horrible. There were more people and more accusations. It was all my fault. All I could see was blood flowing out of my steamer trunks. All I could see was Sammy's head in my hatbox.

On the fourth day, the guards came to get me. They had me get my hat, coat, and purse. We went outside and into a large black car. "Where are we going?" I asked innocently. They said nothing, but as we traveled out of town, I had the sinking feeling they were taking me to Florence and the penitentiary.

"My dress is stuck in the car door," I told them, after we got moving on the street. The car was pulled over and the guard got out of the car, opened the car door, and unsnagged the hem of my dress. A car was approaching and he had to dash back to the car. Somehow in the process, they forgot to lock the door. I stayed quiet. We drove for a long time to a huge building with a gate and spiked fencing. There was some problem with the guard of the gate and my guards. The driver hung out at the gate with the gate guard. The other guard walked up to the big building. "Now is the time," I breathed. I slowly unlatched the car door and scooted, bent over to a long line of bushes. I kept moving until I got to a road intersection. I stood there, wondering what I should do next.

"Hey, pretty lady, ya need a ride?" yelled a guy in a classy white Lincoln sedan.

"Yes," I said looking around. "I need to get back to the station for my one o'clock bus." I looked down to my watch. We had forty-five minutes to get there. I jumped into the car.

"Well, it's too bad you have to leave so early," said the man. I knew what was on his mind.

"It was all my fault," I countered. "I went to see my Uncle Henry at the looney bin and I stayed too long." I figured that would divert his attention to other things and it worked. Within forty minutes, we were through the traffic and at the bus depot. I jumped out before he braked the car and I gave him a silly little wave. I went right in and bought a one-way ticket to California.

Philip (and Anthony)

I named my cat "Schitzy." She was two cats in one. She seemed nervous or loving, one or the other, most of the time. Anthony named his cat "Harrington." He claimed it was because some day the cat was going to be the King of England. "And because he's Harry, get it? *Hairy?*" he chuckled. Anthony was going to be a comedian when he grew up.

We were playing with our cats in the living room with the wooden door open and the screen door shut. I was glancing out the screen door every once in a while, when suddenly a weird thing happened. Anthony went to the kitchen to get the cat food and a black car stopped in front of our house. A man that looked like a doctor got out and went around the car. He opened the car door and was ripping at some material. Harrington went crazy and ran at the screen door. In one fell swoop, he forcefully jumped heavily, rattling the door. He hung onto the screen, ripping and tearing it. Schitzy also sensed something. She tensed all up. The sheer weight of the big cat and a slight wind swung the door open and Harrington flew out. At the same time, another car almost ran over the doctor guy as he scrambled to get in the car. At the same time, I shouted "Anthony! Harrington got out!" He ran in to see, scattering cat food all across the floor. I held my cat to my chest. Anthony ran right out the door and looked and called everywhere, but we never saw Harrington again.

Schitzy lived another summer and then got sick and died. Winnie Ruth Judd worked in California for six years before they found her and they put her back in the Phoenix Asylum. Winnie Ruth Judd died in her sleep on October 23, 1998 at the age of ninety-three.

The Desert Full Moon

November 19, 2021

Rising up in her glory.
Crown Queen gleams o'er towering mountains.
She swoops like a spotlight.
Casting moon glow below.
The desert is silent,
As deer herds wander, through brushy Palo Verde.
Nibbling tender sprouts from the tips of the trees.
Soft high lights cast shadows into deep dark washes.
Where wily Javelinas kick up their hooved feet.
O'r sand flats, the coyotes are snaking 'round grease wood.
They are taking,
As they scurry around with a very sharp eye.
Out of nowhere there's a darting, a pouncing, a parting,
And the coyotes rejoice and lift their howls high.
Queen moon keeps drifting to a haze that is misting,
Clouds caress and dress her to dip 'round the world,
For another night date.
Everything in sight drowned in soft light.
Astounded saguaros loom big and so real.
Then Moon Queen drops down to the flat line of ground,
As red, rosy sun pops his fine fiery head.

THE WALL

B. Bob and Sam Roy lived in a pretty nice manufactured house on Dog Patch Road. Over the years, they had been robbed three times, so they built a concrete and steel wall around their place, The Wall had a remote-control gate made of steel. It was a marvel of technology.

Just at rooster's crow, around 4:00 a.m., the men were sleepily getting ready to go out to a job site. They were in the middle of another wall project. It was a cool day and it looked like it might rain. B. Bob had the truck running. Roy came out of the house juggling two mini coolers filled with lunch. They got settled in the cab and B. Bob punched the button on the remote. He mashed it a couple of times. Roy looked over and said, "I think your batteries are dead, B. Bobb."

"Well, if that don't beat all," sighed B. Bob. He handed Roy the remote and Roy went back into the mobile home to get fresh batteries. He rushed out to the porch and he trips, knocking the remote out of his hand and down an oversized stick squirrel hole between the concrete and the dirt.

B Bob turned off the truck. "Well, if *that* don't beat all!" he grumbled. He gets out as Roy scoured around in the hole. "Ouch!" he yelped. "Something just bit me!" he held up his fingers. One was bloody.

B. Bob waxed eloquently, "We are trapped like rats in our making."

"It's all your fault, B. Bob," whined Roy. "You are the one who just had to build this wall."

"Well, you didn't complain very much after the third time we got robbed," said B. Bob in a low voice. He marched over the garage to get a long ladder. He proceeded to climb over the iron gate. B. Bob was getting rather portly in middle age. He got half-way on the ladder and the ladder started to bend with a creak in the middle, slowly into the wall. Now the ladder slammed on the ground with a loud "carn-sarn nit" and B. Bob marched to the garage. He wheeled out the portable welder to cut the fence open.

By this time, as the men were busy solving their problem, they did not pay attention to the fact that the day was not getting lighter. It was getting darker in all directions as billowing clouds were looming over the Tucson Mountains to several thousand feet. The clouds looked like thunderheads on top and heavy rain clouds on the bottom. They were not moving anywhere, but up.

Roy, feeling trapped, scaled the cinder block wall, getting all scratched up on the rough surface. He ended up losing his balance and dove over the wall, mostly to avoid a cholla cactus on the other side. "I'm bleeding all over," whimpered Roy. B. Bob, throwing the bent ladder over the wall for Roy to scale.

"Here ya go, Buddy. I'm sorry we are having such a problem," said B. Bob.

Roy grunted as he balanced himself on top of the wall for the second time. B. Bob starts welding a line to make a hole in the steel gate. Then B. Bob's phone rang. It was the boss.

"What's wrong, fellers?" asked his boss.

B. Bob cleared his throat. "Uh, well, we are having trouble with the remote gate opener. Uh, it's stuck," he lied.

The boss started laughing. "Well at least you didn't get it down a rabbit hole. Get down here soon. It's starting to rain and we need to button up this build for a while."

Back to the welding job, B. Bob cuts a rectangular hole in the solid iron gate. He forgot what he is doing as he guided the cut with perfection with his gas-powered unit. If he could only go on with this task, it would be a joy. Welding and

torch cutting were his favorite things to do. He would much rather be making gates than walls. He heaved a sigh as he put the welding unit away in the garage and locked it.

B. Bob started up the truck again. Roy gets in. They stare at the hole in the gate. It was too small for the truck. B. Bob muttered, "I would tell you to get out the bulldozer, but the boss has the key." B. Bob gets out of the truck and, again, gets out the welder.

Suddenly, the gate opened on its own. B. Bob and Roy turned around. The remote popped out of the hole and Roy grabbed it, just as an irate stick squirrel scurries out of the hole, cheeping wildly.

"Yes!" shouted B. Bob as he did a little dance and got in the truck. "We did it!" he drove it out on the street. Roy got in. Then B. Bob looked in the rearview mirror. The gate was closed and now there is a big window cut out of it.

"Well, if *that don't* beat all! We can't go gally-vanting out with a hole cut that big in the gate!" B. Bob turned off the engine and got out of the truck. He paced in front of the gate and mumbled, "That don't beat all . . . That don't beat all."

Roy gets out of the truck and looks around and then sighed, "Look, B. Bob, do you see anyone down this street?" (A roadrunner crosses the orange clay road which is now getting hit by big splats of rain.) "Okay, other than that bird, there is no one there. Do you think that for one day, we could leave the hole there in the gate? No one can get in with a truck to get out anything big."

B. Bob looked stern. "No. We had those robberies."

Roy pointed to the gate. "The gate is locked. The house is locked and the garage is locked. Let's go to work."

B. Bob shook his head. "Someone is watching. We don't know who is watching, but someone is watching for the right moment to pick us off again." B. Bob had clouds smoldering in his eyes.

Roy looked up and down the road. "You mean the old man with no stomach? You mean the weak old lady in the wheelchair? Or that little old bent granny and grandpa across from us? I seriously don't think any of them could haul off much even in six hours."

B. Bob shook his head.

Roy tried to talk some sense, "I think we have done enough damage for today. If it would make it any better, I could ask the neighbors to watch the place while we are gone."

Bob shook his head. "Only commies and socialists would do such a thing. We gotta stand guard. What if one of those convoys or caravans from Mexico comes marching in and takes over the place? What if they get our papers for the truck?"

"Well, if it would make you feel better, go get them," sighed Roy. B. Bob steps into the hole in the gate and stomps up onto the porch. He unlocked the door and went in.

Again, huge splatters of rain pelted down, followed by wheezing gusts of wind. For the first time Roy noticed that the sky was covered with big towering clouds, He smelled the rain, the wet clay smell that fills the desert. He looked at his watch. 11:30. Yes, they had been preoccupied ever since 5:00 a.m. with the big gate problem. Neither of the men had noticed the approaching storm.

Roy's phone rang, or rather mooed, because of his ring tone. It was the boss.

"Hey, Roy, there's no reason for you two to come to the work site. It's been raining heavy here for twenty minutes and the road down here is flooding. See you tomorrow early, okay? Like around 6:00 a.m. You and Bob can just sit tight."

Bob came back with a fist full of papers and jumped in the truck. Roy got in beside him as the wind pelted hail at the window. "I just got a call from the boss," yelled Roy. "The worksite is flooding and I think the storm is coming our way."

Suddenly a huge gust of wind rocked the Ford F-150. Huge hailstones were crashing down on all sides, just splitting their ears with the sound. Finally, a hard-baseball-size hailstone embedded itself on the driver's side of the windshield. They both jumped in their seats in surprise. The whole window crackles into hundreds of spiderwebs.

Bob pounded the steering wheel and said, "Well, if that don't beat all."

THE UNIQUE CACTUS WREN

(Arizona State Bird)

The cactus wren is a speckled brown bird with bright white eyebrows that extend from the bill, across and above their red eyes, to the sides of the neck. They have pale cinnamon sides and a white chest with dark speckles. The back is brown with heavy white streaks, and the tail is barred white and black—especially noticeable from below. Males and females look alike, but juveniles are slightly paler and have a brown eye.

Unlike other wrens that typically hide in vegetation, the cactus wren seems to have no fear. They perch atop cacti and other shrubs to announce their presence and forage out in the open. They do not cock their tails over their back the way other wrens do. Instead, they fan their tail feathers, flashing their white tail tips.

Cactus wrens are beautiful singers, once they get their airbags in their necks full of air. Their song starts out slow and raspy and quickly thrills. At the end of a song, if there is any air in their jowls, they sound a "cuck cuck" a few times. If there is music, they can even sing along in tune.

They are very precise about building their nests, and they have a lot of competition from Doves and cranky hook-billed thrashers. They will steal eggs and ruin their nests. Cactus wrens are masters of deception by building decoy nests to confuse the thrashers. If the nest is not destroyed, it can be used as a look-out perch or even a nest for the next year.

Cactus wrens range in deserts, arid foothills, coastal sage scrub, and urban areas throughout the Southwest, especially in areas with thorny shrubs, cholla, and prickly pear. Surprisingly, they live seven to ten years and mate for life.

Cactus Wren

Full throated,
Singing us a song.
About the rocks and desert sand,
Laying here so long.
He trills on
About the old ones.
First persons meet Spanish mission.
Clay and rocks baked by suns.
Roughly cackling,
He's vain to complain
About the Calvary men marching
O'er the proud and silent, layin'
Raw-ly calling,
The ravens join the curse.
As settlers dot desert with ranches.
Sour notes are natures' worse.
Cooing breaths,
Doves join in the song.
As whirling branches and whistling trees,
Join a hive of swirling bees. . .
The wind bends limbs down on their knees. . .
Full throated,
Singin us a song.
The cactus wren sings memories
Of a history, oh so long.

BIRD COUNT REPORT: NARRATIVE

February 15, 2022
"Going out to count birds. Wish me cluck!"

Every year when we arrive in Arizona, usually in October, we declare a "Year of the (insert bird or animal)." Once it was "The Year of the Roadrunner." Another time it was "Year of the Lizard." This year it is "The Year of the Hawk."

Since October, 2021, the hawk count has been unusually high. This includes the many varieties from the steel-blue-grey kestrels to the barred hawk, and redtail hawks. They love to drool over the chickens next door to us who have a covered pen. There is a pair of hawks who lick their beaks at the unattainable chickens and hope their weight will collapse the structure.

The barred hawk divebombs the common doves and eyeballs the bunnies. There is a pair of rather old birds and one sharp yearling who brought his mate by the other day. Carl shoots them with a BB Gun because he is defending his large dove population, not to mention the quail, thrashers, wrens, sparrows, cottontail bunnies, and a pair of pigeons. We also have a pair of Inca doves. They show up sporadically. The BB Gun does no more than scare them away when the copper ball bounces off of their hardened feathers. It is just a conditioning effect.

On February 8, 2022, we traveled south of the South Tucson Mountains, on Highway 86 or the Ajo Highway. Just as we got to the little burg of Three Points, I saw four redtail hawks flying north on the west side of the road. Then, as we entered the Tohono O'odham Reservation, I saw two more redtail hawks bouncing on a barbed-wire fence. Their tails glowed red in the sun as they swayed in the breeze. Finally, one lost his balance and hopped to the ground. These two were much larger than chickens: more like large, wild turkeys, but not as skinny.

Just as we approached the Native town of Sells. We see four turkey vultures crowding around a roadkill. They were fluttering their wings, unfolding them like a tent.

The weather was bright, but not too hot as we approached Why. We saw no bird activity, even when we got out to Darby Wells Road and onto Bates Well Road. We set up camp by a wash. We saw a flyover of two crows which possibly were the same pair that hung out around our camp in November, but they did not stay. Every day, we saw a resident hummingbird who was checking out the wolfberry bush in our camp for flowers. No flowers can be seen anywhere and there were very few creatures out as they seem to be in hibernation mode. It has been drier and colder out here near Ajo than it has been in the South Tucson Mountains.

On our second night we heard a coyote checking out our camp and giving us three stars and a good review to his two companions who were not brave enough approach our camp.

We also were swarmed by what looked like honey bees in the heat of the day. We built a campfire to repel them a bit. They smelled our water and meat. We decided to leave our camp. The wind came up and I did not see any more birds on the way home.

CRISIS IN DOG PATCH

(Allegorically Speaking)
February 23–March 2, 2022

Pitbull was a lonely animal who lived in a huge two-and-a-half-acre yard. He had everything he could possibly want: a water dish, food dish, and dog house. The rest of the dogs and humans milled around and ignored him, even though he was the alpha dog. He was the supreme leader, keeping to himself because of the sickness.

One day, Pitbull dug out of his yard to look around. He found out that across the street, there was a yard with some of the dogs that used to be in his yard. *Why were they there?* He thought. He had just assumed they all simply died. That was not the case.

He looked over the wire fence. The yard was clean, but small. There was a swimming pool, a chicken yard, and several dog condos scattered around in tastefully kept gardens.

His pallid face turned raging red as he limped back to his large yard.

Pitbull did not sleep that night. Before sun-up, he started howling outside his dog house. No one would listen to him. No one would bark back. So, he went up the street to the toughest dogs on the dirt road— The Hounds of War. They all had the markings of Doberman, with a touch of Russian shepherd. They were kept as fighting dogs for the casino.

Just at sunrise, after listening to Pitbull tell the history of Dogpatch, The Hounds of War agreed to help. They proposed to break down the fence at the nice yard, striking in the dead of night. "I will go with you!" howled Pitbull, but that night he decided to catch up on his sleep.

Not only did The Hounds of War break down the fence, but they dog-bombed the lawn and torched the chicken coop. There was roasted chicken for all and the Hounds figured they could blame the disaster on the coyotes.

To make a long story short, the Dog Patch community started to question Pitbull's sanity. Did he fall off the roof of his doghouse after one of his history lectures? Did his tongue tie, shutting off blood to his brain while he talked of fascists, holocaust, genocide? Or maybe it was the golden glow, radiating off the orange baby balloon, always floating on the horizon? Whatever.

The dogs (and even the cats!) of his own yard staged protests of his actions. Over a thousand dogs, cats, bunnies, and birds were jailed and sentenced to fifteen years hard labor. The next day even more were jailed including three donkeys and seven goats. Pitbull proclaimed, "I never knew there were so many animals in this yard!"

Meanwhile, in the pretty little yard, the Collie Dogs built a rock island in the swimming pool. Just at sunset, The Dogs of War came by on patrol and ordered the group off the island. The Collie Captain barked, "Awww, go bite me!" and his minions laughed with glee. The Dogs of War rolled their cannon around the house and blew them up to smithereens.

Later that night, The Dogs of War brought Pitbull to the pretty little yard, now with two burned out spots: the chicken coop and the swimming pool.

"Good work, you dogs," Pitbull growled.

Days turned into weeks, and weeks turned to months, and months turned into years. That is how it is with war.

Pitbull stayed in his doghouse most of the time, except to get his dog chow and water. Each and every day he would see a delegation of animals which stood twenty feet away begging him to stop the war. Many of the animals from the pretty yard were moving back to the big yard.

One day a goat stepped over the twenty-foot borderline and got right into Pitbull's face. "If you really want the pretty little yard, g-g-g-g-go over there. There is n-n-n-n-n-no r-r-r-r-r-rooom for you here. This place is so crowded we can't even play k-k-k-k-kick the can!"

"Kill this goat!" barked Pitbull.

But there were no toadies to do his bidding.

So Pitbull strolled over to the pretty little yard—head held high-tail in the air—it was time to take possession of this land that he worked so hard to get. It was time for him to take his rightful place. When he got there, he hardly recognized it! All the bushy green trees were torn apart. The land was barren and very hot. A huge burned-out tank occupied the front yard. Several Dogs of War were lounging on top of it.

"What happened? The yard is not pretty anymore and all the animals are gone!" howled Pitbull.

"War happened," snapped the head Dog of War. He hopped off the top of the truck as his minions chuckled quietly. The Dog of War general showed Pitbull around to the backyard which was unrecognizable. It looked like a parking lot of burned-out trucks, jeeps, rocket launchers, and tanks. The wild desert plants and tasteful landscaping were gone. All the dog condos were flattened under the war machinery and the swimming pool was a blackened pit.

"I can't live in a place like this," moaned Pitbull.

"Why not?" said the head Dog of War. "I've been here two years now and. .

"What are you doing here?" shrieked a human lady holding a big broom. She stood on a set of crushed porch steps tilted at different angles. The awning was dangling from two boards. Suddenly she leapt gracefully off the porch and started chasing Pitbull and the head Dog of War. The other dogs heard the commotion and raced to be part of the action. The Babushka swung the broom around battering the dogs from all angles, leaping from one blackened vehicle to another, jumping down to the ground, and vaulting broken concrete and tree branches. She cracked her broom over Pitbull's head stopping him for a moment and breaking the broom handle off. She threw it down and said, "Before I came out here, I called animal control to put you away for all these war crimes! They are here now."

With that, a crew of animal control personnel lassoed the dogs with a wide garrot of wire that snapped shut on the dog's necks. They fought, but the loop was attached to a big stick which helped guide or drag the animals to a truck.

"Good riddance!" shouted the Babushka.

The next day, several tow-trucks pulled all the war machines out of the yard. The ground was tilled and seeds and native plants were placed all around before the monsoon rains came over the sky. A few weeks later, the sun appeared and desert wildflowers and sunflowers bloomed across the land.

CONCEALED CARRY

May 21, 2013

We blew through Parker, Arizona at the state border at 3:00 a.m. It was already getting to be way too hot to be in the desert even at the end of March, but we had obligations to make an appearance in Tucson this weekend for the Cancer Walk at the park. Bart and I were "Walking Across America" for cancer, so we were part of the show. We had a big interview in Barstow just three days ago which was lots of fun with a banjo picker and a fiddler. A couple of cowboys hit on me and I was so glad to have Bart by my side. Bart broke his silence and said, "Gee, Becky, be careful with that smile o' you'r-un! We are now in the heart of the Wild West from here on out. Men prey on happy girls like you."

So as soon as we passed Running Man Gas, we were out of town and headed for Bouse where Bart's grandma lived. We were going to spend the night and get off early to connect with I-10 and then take the cut-off. We were climbing out of the Colorado River valley and so we would walk up a hill, then walk down a hill. Up a hill and down a hill. On and on, past the Fairgrounds intersection. Down a long steep curve. Up at the top of the next hill, in the distance, we could see a man standing on the side of the road. He walked right into the center of the road.

I squinted and said, "What is that guy doing, Bart?"

"I'm purty sure he is at the Quartzite intersection. Maybe he's hitch'en a ride there or to Bouse."

By now it was almost 6:00 a.m. and the dawn was splashing the sky with muted light. This hill was the longest and steepest of all the ones before. The mountains were blushing ever so slightly. The sun popped his head up over a far mountain.

We could hear the man yelling from the middle of the road. "Slow down. Slow down. Perfect!"

Suddenly, the first of the refer trucks of the day came whizzing by and the man had to dive off the road and into a ditch. I turned to Bart, "Do you think that man is crazy?"

"Uh, well 'crazy is as crazy does' so let's just watch out for him," said Bart.

He examined the man as we walked closer. "I'd say he is packing heat, Becky."

The man was climbing out of the ditch and put his white cowboy hat back on his head. He dusted himself off and yelled, "Perfect! Yeah! Stand still, yeah right there." We froze for a minute, watching him and keeping our distance. He started fumbling with his bag at this side and pulled out something.

We looked at each other and Bart said, "If'n you hear a pop, dive for the ditch just like he did." Bart watched the guy carefully. I slowly sidestepped over to the ditch. He held a big black something right up to his face, but he was talking to us the whole time.

"Come on kids, keep walking. That's right. Slow and easy. Keep coming! Good one!"

The guy with the gun said, "Come on, come on keep walking. Walk faster. Good!"

We obediently walked forward. We were getting close. Bart could not stand it and blurted, "Why the heck do you want us to come forward? Shoot us now!"

"I am I am!" said the guy as he moved around with the black thing in front of his face. "I saw you guys on TV last night and I knew you was 'a commin' out this way. I wanna shoot you!"

Bart jumped in his boots when he said this and I was trembling all over. The man was fumbling with his bag with his thick, swollen, mechanic's hands, and I looked around for a place to hide. There was not a rock, bush, or even a cactus to get behind.

"Keep walking. Just act natural," said the man. We kept moving. We were ten feet away.

He shouted, "There, now, look up and smile!" Now we could see that he had a camera! He was a photographer and he showed us our photos. We took pictures of us with him and exchanged cards.

"Thank you, kids!" The photographer yelled and waved in back of himself, as old men do now-a-days. He headed down the hill towards Quartzite. There was his car parked safely out of the way. We moved out of the intersection and found some boulders to sit on.

Bart was sweating profusely. "Man," said Bart. "I thought we was gonna be goners, Becky. Wha'd I tell you about being careful. We are really in the Wild West!"

SMOKE SIGNALS

Cochise descended the rubble of rock which today we call his stronghold. His people were camped across the valley in the high mountains for the summer. Soon he would have to move his people to the stronghold for the winter, away from the brutal high icy peaks. His people were at Turkey Canyon, hunting for the winter larder. The thought of roasted turkey made his mouth water. "Tazhii," (turkey) he muttered under his breath.

Running Boy was his companion for this trip and he was busying himself gathering dead branches and tufts of grass as they walked the trail. He would gather them and leave them in strategic places to haul these bundles further up the trail. He sprinted out ahead of Cochise, grabbed a pile of grass and carried it past the chief up the hill to his next landing then hustled down the path dragging an overlooked limb. This amused Cochise so much that he gathered some dead limbs too. Running Boy was a good choice for this project.

The next day, the pair took a tour of the horse trail and pasture on the north side of this mountain. It would be a good winter for the animals with the grass waving tall in the breeze. They climbed out of the pasture and into the craggy rocks where they rested for the day. A few times, Cochise rose and gazed across the valley. His eyes shifted from the Dragoon Mountain ridge to the towering Chiricahua mountains. In between was the Sulphur Springs Valley and the mysterious dry lake of the playa.

If you were looking directly at Cochise, you would think he was asleep. His shrouded eye lids drooped as was the case of all elders who had seen too much in their lives. Suddenly, his eyes popped open as he saw a line of dust far to the northeast. The line of dust came from the north, traveling the high mountains of the east. The line fanned out a bit and the dust devils grew high over the flat land below. Running Boy saw it too and moved to his side. "Daadatlijende" (whiteman), he spat out. They were men all in blue coats on horses. Lazily, the line of dust drifted in the wind.

DESERT REPORT

Cochise pointed to the other side of the rock outcropping and pointed to Running Boy. He placed his hand on his chest and pointed down and again to the other side. He handed Running Boy the flint pouch and said, "Ch'ighah" (go). He would get coals from their camp fire to light his own fire. They swiftly scrambled to their locations.

At the kitchen camp, Cochise gingerly placed hot coals on a flat rock and carried them up the east side of the hill. He went halfway up to a rocky point where Running Boy had been preparing the site for many days. There was grass from the playa, brush, and heavy limbs. There was also an antelope stomach bag full of water dripping slowly into the piles of grass. Swiftly, Cochise dumped the burning coals on the rock ledge and plopped a bundle of wet grass on top. Then he made a second one. *Two columns of smoke spoke of danger, halfway up the hill, meant the danger was not right away, but to be on alert.*

The bundles smoldered right away and puffs of smoke shot into the sky. Before the grass caught aflame, he took two sticks and carefully lifted the grass bundle off the fire, turned, grabbed another bundle of grass and set it on the fire.

Meanwhile, from a rocky ledge above Turkey Canyon, two braves were lounging on a warn rock. Suddenly, they saw the smoke and the runner took off for the camp below, to warn the camp.

Cochise placed a third grass bundle when he saw a column of smoke from Running Boy, above. He took the bundle off the fire because he felt that the lookouts had been alerted. After that, he stashed the smoldering grass between some rocks and wet it cold. He started up the hill toward Running Boy. By the time he got to him, there were two fires wafting smoke to the south in the direction of Turkey Canyon. Running Boy went to lookout on the east side of the mountain to see where the blue coats were. The line of dust was not heading south, but now northeast to Fort Bowie. After making sure, he ran back around the hill to tell Cochise, who had three fires going by now. They quickly extinguished their fires and neatened up the area. By the time they got back to their base camp, it was night.

The next day, Cochise lit the fire at the ledge halfway up the hill. He kept it going all day, to say that all the danger was over. Running Boy kept vigil on the valley.

There were no more threats and soon the rest of the tribe started to cautiously trickle in to the stronghold. The oak trees turned golden at the sight of the people coming back. Winter would soon be upon them with icy cold mornings and sunny afternoons. There they would stay in their rocky fortress in those last golden days. Little did they know, very soon, it would be their last winter camp.

"Ted" Ettore DeGrazia: Arizona Cultural Hero

Degrazia rolled this jalopy down into the wash in back of his house and harvested wood for the winter.

What is a cultural hero? What does it mean to eat and breathe a culture, both from within one's self, and to be perceived from the outside as having this quality? A recent example is Oprah Winfrey, who not only represents her own heritage and gender, but the entire nation as well for the late twentieth and twenty-first century. Arizona is a unique blending pot with many Native Americans, Mexicans, Okies from Oklahoma, Spanish peoples, and immigrants from the old world who came to work in the mines. These people make up the foundation for the state each one building upon the culture of Arizona.

The life of Ettore DeGrazia was cultural example of the Southwest, the heritage of the "Wild West," and the culture of the Native Americans, Mexicans, and immigrants who came to make a new life in this country. He was born to Italian immigrants on June 14, 1909 in the mining camp of Morenci, in what was then Arizona Territory. Being in a mining community, he grew up with many immigrants of different nationalities and the natives of the area. He roamed the desert and mountains collecting rocks and learning the lore of the land. He had an urge as a child to make art.

When he was barely eleven, the mine closed down and his parents decided to return to Calabria, Italy with their seven children. There, in Italy, he was exposed to music and was in the town band, playing the trumpet. He also saw many examples of classical art all around him. In 1925, the mine in Arizona reopened and the family returned to America. Ettore had to relearn English and so he was placed in a first grade class. His teacher nicknamed him Ted and the name stuck with him the rest of his life.

Back in America, Ted tried mining, but the underground life was not for him. He hitched a ride to the University of Arizona in Tucson with fifteen dollars and his trumpet in 1933 and supported himself by planting trees at the university and leading a band at night. He married Alexandra Diamos in 1936 and moved to Bisbee so that Ted DeGrazia could manage his father-in-law's Lyric Theater, owned by the family. They had three children during this time, but were divorced in 1946.

Ted DeGrazia's dream was to be an artist. He became focused with this goal in about 1941, painting scenes of Bisbee. The magazine, *Arizona Highways*, picked up some of his work. On a holiday to Mexico with Alexandra, the couple ditched the ballet at intermission and walked down the street where muralist Diego Rivera was working. This meeting resulted in an offer to DeGrazia to become an intern and work with Rivera and Jose Clemente Orozco.

Later, with such a background, one would think that the arts community in Tucson would welcome such an artist back home, but that was not the case. The only thing to do was to open a studio and keep working. With twenty-five dollars down, he bought an acre at Prince Road and Campbell Avenue in Tucson, to build a studio. He also went back to the University to receive a BA in education and a BFA and master of arts with a thesis paper of a very futuristic study of art and music. All this was accomplished by 1944. New York Sculptor, Marion Sheret met DeGrazia at his Campbell Ave. Studio. Their view of art and life were matched and they married in Mexico in 1947.

The emigrants of the Dust Bowl of Oklahoma were arriving to the town of Tucson and the artists were getting crowded out of their community. They decided to buy a ten-acre site in the early 1950s to build a new art center with living quarters, studio, and the "Gallery in the Sun."

We arrived at the DeGrazia Compound on January 17, 2018. My companions were both "good old Arizonian boys." Carl Reynolds graduated from Amphi High School in 1956 and Bill Cox who used to prepare canvases for DeGrazia. We entered the main gallery, finished in 1965, which opens with iron gates which are replica of the Yuma Territorial Prison gate.

Deer dancing ceremony.

A true renaissance man, DeGrazia experimented with oil paintings, sculptures, ceramics, and watercolors. He collected local art and artifacts. He even worked with fabrics, jewelry, found art, and natural objects to capture the spirit of the Southwest and the divergent people of the area. All of these things can be seen in the main gallery located at 6300 North Swan, Tucson, Arizona. To live what you know every day and to break the standard rules of art to capture his view of the southwest was important. He also did not ignore the heritage of the Mexican and other South American peoples. He delved into the history of the Spanish explorers and notably Father Kino, the Catholic Missionary and Cabeza DeVaca, a doomed gold-seeking exploiter. He also was privileged to know and become friends with the Papago and Yaqui Natives. Their spring celebration which paralleled the Christian Easter celebration, was a subject of many wonderful paintings and artifacts. The Deer Dance is depicted in several gatherings in his paintings. He also collected some of the Deer Dance artifacts. It is an overwhelming collection.

A "Los Ninos" painting owned by the Good Family.

In the 1950s and early 1960s, National Geographic, and NBC highlighted his art and UNICEF chose his 1957 painting "Los Ninos" for their 1960 holiday card. In thanks, as a regional tradition, Ted DeGrazia built an adobe chapel. Sadly, on May 29, 2017, a candle got too hot near the altar and part of the mural-filled mission burned down. Now the gallery board and staff are struggling to put the building back together. Most of the murals will have to be restored. The adobe building took Ted and his Yaqui friends two years to build. It opened in 1952.

Ted DeGrazia died of cancer on September 17, 1982 at the age of seventy-three. His entire compound of galleries, the house, and Mission are listed on the National Historic Registry as a historic district in 2006. Prints of DeGrazia's work are still being sold on eBay for hundreds to thousands of dollars. Out back of the mission, Ted DeGrazia's grave is marked with the stones from the Morenci Mine. The Catholic Mission, Deer Dancer in the garden, brilliant colors of the Gallery in the Sun, the moving rodeo cowboys, and the desert landscape with galloping conquistadores and missionaries, all paint a picture of the American Southwest heritage and the lands beyond the border.

For travelers not familiar with the Southwest, a visit to the DeGrazia Gallery in the Sun in Tucson, Arizona would be valuable to know the culture of the Southwest. Ted DeGrazia is cultural hero of the southwest as his art reflects the mixture of cultures which call Tucson their home.

DESERT REPORT

Desert Gems

Glowing jewels in desert sand.
The cactus flowers make a stand.
Their iridescent petals glow
As bees buzz in, and to, and fro.
The yellow pollen dusts their dress
Of red and yellow, orange and gold,
No less.
Hotly comes the sun at dawn.
Bright petals glow, and then they're gone.

The Solar Farm

We met near a high iron gate that entered into a dirt road, which led to an adobe shack at the end. We were reporters from various media organizations to witness one of the first solar farms in the area. The "farmer" opened the gate to let us in then he chained it shut. He had a big, wide straw hat, like I see the migrants use out in the lettuce fields near Yuma. He wore leather gloves and started handing out cardboard sunglasses to everyone. At first, I did not see a single solar panel, until we passed the adobe shack and started down a hill. There in a bowl of the canyon below was acres and acres of panels. We noticed orange signs on the farm and in the distance near the highway warning people to not look out at the sea of glass for too long. Some of the vain reporters finally slipped on their glasses.

"What is that over there? Is that a lake?" asked one of the young reporters.

"No lake, ma'm," said our guide. "That's just a twenty-first-century mirage of more solar panels."

An older reporter asked, "What kinds of problems happen out here that surprised you?"

"Weeds and grass." said the farmer. "After our first monsoon we discovered that we had a real shade problem, with the panels, creating more weeds and grass than you have ever seen. At first, we tried to mow them down, but there was a lot of problems just keeping up with the mowing and hitting rocks which broke the glass. So, then we got some goats, but they just trampled down the grass. Then we got some sheep and that worked really slick. I never thought I'd have to hire a shepherd, but I did."

A young lady with her phone on a recording application asked "So what is the history of this place?"

"We are in the center of Borlach Ranch. This was once a nine-thousand-acre cattle ranch. The adobe building, we passed was the ranch house back in 1880. Our eight-thousand panel solar farm produces ten megawatts of power, daily. The panels are grouped in solar arrays and are powered by Tesla battery cells."

A skeptical reporter gazed across the land covered with glass panels. "So you have these eight-thousand glass power-catchers. How many houses down in Phoenix does that power?"

"Today, we will power three-hundred-and-seventy-THOUSAND homes. In contrast, on a good windy day, only two-hundred-and-fifty-thousand homes will be powered by windfarms," said the solar farmer.

We walked along silently, the sun bearing down rapidly, as we crunched along over the trail. At a high point we paused to take pictures, looking back over the farm, with the ranch house in the background. We came down from the "lookie" and were greeted by a group of sheep who paralleled our hike in the next aisle over between the solar panels. They would baa at people who were too slow. The yearlings bounded back and forth as we walked along. The lead ewe set the pace for the fast walkers and moved us along back to the adobe house again.

The farmer guided us to the back of the house with a high wall. This patio was cool and there were wooden benches everywhere. There was a water cooler and lots of paper cups. "Be sure to hydrate before you leave the solar farm," our leader reminded us. There was a thermometer on an outside pillar and even though it was fall and not even noon, the temperature was already ninety-eight degrees.

"I still don't get it," said a man in a Stetson. "How does the sunlight create the power? Shouldn't we have figured that out a long time ago?"

The solar farmer smiled. "Our Moms figured it long ago. If we place a gallon of water on the table in the sun with some tea bags in it, we get hot tea steeped with tea bags. The same is true in the solar panels. Come on over here to the wall and I will show you these posters about how it works."

Every single person there grabbed their water and sat at the benches like attentive schoolchildren.

The solar farmer pointed at the first poster. "Sunlight hits the glass and photon particles move and stimulate electrons of silicon atoms in the solar cells."

"It's like a science experiment in a Petri dish!" blurted out the man in the Stetson.

The solar farmer beamed. "The ultimate science experiment of physics but not biology."

The solar farmer moved to the next poster. "These solar cells move the electrical currents. The electrical current flows into an inverter which changes DC (direct current) to AC (alternating currents) which move along the copper wires in a sort of wandering cycle that can be on and then off. Unused electricity flows to a utility meter here on the grounds or out to the power grid. There is a give and take of energy: some stored in batteries, some on the meter, and onto the grid."

"It is so magical—we can't even see it," said the reporter with the recording phone.

"And yet we do," grinned the solar farmer. "We see it every time we flip on a light or charge our phone battery. We do see the results, but we also take this science for granted. Any more questions?" asked the solar farmer. There were none, but he passed out his business card with his email on it just in case.

We approached the entrance and a roadrunner crossed our path. "There is our lucky bird," laughed the solar farmer. He led us out to the gate in the blazing sun which will soon be transformed into electricity to power our world.

Printed in the USA
CPSIA information can be obtained
at www.ICGtesting.com
LVHW010340150224
771723LV00002B/30